Puppy Mudge Loves His Blanket

Puppy Mudge Loves His Blanket

By Cynthia Rylant

Illustrated by Isidre Mones

in the style of Suçie Stevenson

SCHOLASTIC INC.

New York Toronto London Auckland Sydney
Mexico City New Delhi Hong Kong Buenos Aires

ISBN 0-439-56136-1

Text copyright © 2004 by Cynthia Rylant. Illustrations copyright © 2004 by Suçie Stevenson. All rights reserved. Published by Scholastic Inc., 557 Broadway, New York, NY 10012, by arrangement with Simon & Schuster Books for Young Readers, Simon & Schuster Children's Publishing Division. SCHOLASTIC and associated logos are trademarks and/or registered trademarks of Scholastic Inc.

12 11 10 9 8 7 6 5 4 3 2 1   4 5 6 7 8 9/0

Printed in the U.S.A.   23

First Scholastic printing, September 2004

Book design by Mark Siegel
The text for this book is set in Goudy.
The illustrations are rendered in pen-and-ink and watercolor.

This is Mudge.
He is Henry's puppy.

Mudge has a blanket.

Mudge LOVES his blanket.

He sleeps on it.

He hides under it.

He takes it places.

Sometimes he loses it.

Where is Mudge's blanket now?

Henry looks on the chair.

Mudge looks on the chair.
No blanket.

Henry looks under the bed.
Mudge looks under the bed.

No blanket.

Mudge is so sleepy.
He needs his blanket.

Mudge sniffs.

He sniffs and sniffs and sniffs.

Good Mudge!
He sniffed all the way . . .

to his blanket!

Now he can rest.

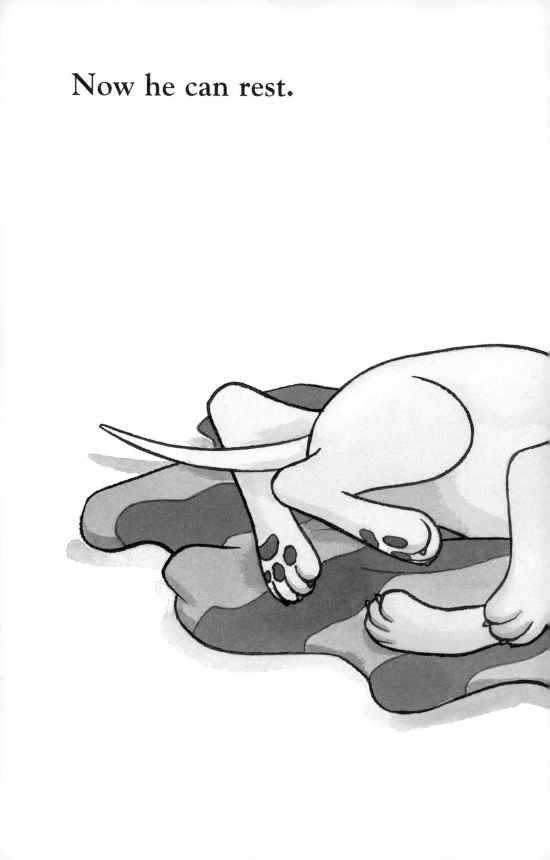